The
Inner
Room

Faber
Stories

Robert Fordyce Aickman was born in 1914 in London. He was married to Edith Ray Gregorson from 1941 to 1957. In 1946 the couple, along with Tom and Angela Rolt, set up the Inland Waterways Association to preserve the canals of Britain. It was in 1951 that Aickman, in collaboration with Elizabeth Jane Howard, published his first ghost stories in a volume entitled *We Are For the Dark*. Aickman went on to publish seven more volumes of 'strange stories' as well as two novels and two volumes of autobiography.

Robert Aickman

The Inner Room

Faber Stories

ff

First published in this single edition in 2019
by Faber & Faber Limited
The Bindery, 51 Hatton Garden
London EC1N 8HN
First published by Faber in *The Wine-Dark Sea* in 2008

Typeset by Faber & Faber Limited
Printed and bound by CPI Group (UK) Ltd, Croydon, CR0 4YY

The right of Robert Aickman to be identified as author of this work
has been asserted in accordance with Section 77 of the Copyright,
Designs and Patents Act 1988

A CIP record for this book
is available from the British Library

ISBN 978-0-571-35177-0

Printed and bound in the UK on FSC® certified paper in line with our continuing
commitment to ethical business practices, sustainability and the environment.
For further information see faber.co.uk/environmental-policy

10 9 8 7 6 5 4 3

It was never less than half an hour after the engine stopped running that my father deigned to signal for succour. If in the process of breaking down, we had climbed, or descended, a bank, then first we must all exhaust ourselves pushing. If we had collided, there was, of course, a row. If, as had happened that day, it was simply that, while we coasted along, the machinery had ceased to churn and rattle, then my father tried his hand as a mechanic. That was the worst contingency of all; at least it was the worst one connected with motoring.

I had learned by experience that neither rain nor snow made much difference, and certainly not fog; but that afternoon it was hotter than any day I could remember. I realised later that it was the famous Long Summer of 1921, when the water at the bottom of cottage wells turned salt, and when eels were found baked and edible in their mud. But to know this at the time, I should have had to read the papers, and though, through my mother's devotion, I had the trick of reading before my third birthday, I mostly left the practice to my younger brother, Constantin. He was reading now from a pudgy volume, as thick as it was broad, and resembling his own head in size and proportion. As always, he had resumed his studies immediately the bumping of our almost springless car permitted, and even before motion had ceased. My mother sat in the front seat inevitably correcting pupils' exercises. By teaching her native German in five schools at once, three of them distant, one of them fashionable, she surprisingly managed to maintain the four of us, and even our car. The front offside door of the car leaned dangerously open into the seething highway.

'I say,' cried my father.

The young man in the big yellow racer shook his head as he tore by. My father had addressed the least appropriate car on the road.

'I say.'

I cannot recall what the next car looked like, but it did not stop.

My father was facing the direction from which we had come, and sawing the air with his left arm, like a very inexperienced policeman. Perhaps no one stopped because all thought him eccentric. Then a car going in the opposite direction came to a standstill behind my father's back. My father perceived nothing. The motorist sounded his horn. In those days, horns squealed, and I covered my ears with my hands. Between my hands and my head my long fair hair was like brittle flax in the sun.

My father darted through the traffic. I think it was the Portsmouth Road. The man in the other car got out and came to us. I noticed his companion, much younger and in a cherry-coloured cloche, begin to deal with her nails.

'Broken down?' asked the man. To me it seemed obvious, as the road was strewn with bits of the engine and oozy blobs of oil. Moreover, surely my father had explained?

'I can't quite locate the seat of the trouble,' said my father.

The man took off one of his driving gauntlets, big and dirty.

3

'Catch hold for a moment.' My father caught hold.

The man put his hand into the engine and made a casual movement. Something snapped loudly.

'Done right in. If you ask me, I'm not sure she'll ever go again.'

'Then I don't think I'll ask you,' said my father affably. 'Hot, isn't it?' My father began to mop his tall corrugated brow, and front-to-back ridges of grey hair.

'Want a tow?'

'Just to the nearest garage.' My father always spoke the word in perfect French.

'Where to?'

'To the nearest car repair workshop. If it would not be troubling you too much.'

'Can't help myself now, can I?'

From under the backseat in the other car, the owner got out a thick, frayed rope, black and greasy as the hangman's. The owner's friend simply said, 'Pleased to meet you,' and began to replace her scalpels and enamels in their cabinet. We jolted towards the town we had traversed an hour or two before; and were then untied outside a garage on the outskirts.

'Surely it is closed for the holiday?' said my mother. Hers is a voice I can always recall upon an instant: guttural, of course, but beautiful, truly golden.

''Spect he'll be back,' said our benefactor, drawing in his rope like a fisherman. 'Give him a bang.' He kicked three times very loudly upon the dropped iron shutter. Then without another word he drove away.

It was my birthday, I had been promised the sea, and I began to weep. Constantin, with a fretful little wriggle, closed further into himself and his book; but my mother leaned over the front seat of the car and opened her arms to me. I went to her and sobbed on the shoulder of her bright red dress.

'Kleine Lene, wir stecken schön in der Tinte.'

My father, who could pronounce six languages perfectly but speak only one of them, never liked my mother to use her native tongue within the family. He rapped more sharply on the shutter. My mother knew his ways, but, where our welfare was at stake, ignored them.

'Edgar,' said my mother, 'let us give the children presents. Especially my little Lene.' My tears, though childish, and less viscous than those shed in later life, had turned the scarlet shoulder of her dress to purple. She squinted smilingly sideways at the damage.

My father was delighted to defer the decision about what next to do with the car. But, as pillage was possible, my mother took with her the exercises, and Constantin his fat little book.

We straggled along the main road, torrid, raucous, adequate only for a gentler period of history. The grit and dust stung my face and arms and knees, like granulated glass. My mother and I went first, she holding my hand. My father struggled to walk at her other side, but for most of the way, the path was too narrow. Constantin mused along in the rear, abstracted as usual.

'It is true what the papers say,' exclaimed my father. 'British roads were never built for motor traffic. Beyond the odd car, of course.'

My mother nodded and slightly smiled. Even in the lineless hopsacks of the twenties, she could not ever but look magnificent, with her rolling, turbulent, honey hair, and Hellenic proportions. Ultimately we reached the High Street. The very first shop had one of its windows stuffed with toys; the other being stacked with groceries and draperies and coal-hods, all dingy. The name POPULAR BAZAAR, in wooden relief as if glued on in building blocks, stretched across the whole front, not quite centre.

It was not merely an out-of-fashion shop, but a shop that at the best sold too much of what no one wanted. My father comprehended the contents of the Toy Department window with a single, anxious glance, and said, 'Choose whatever you like. Both of you. But look very carefully first. Don't hurry.' Then he turned away and began to hum a fragment from 'The Lady of the Rose'.

But Constantin spoke at once. 'I choose those telegraph wires.' They ranged beside a line of tin railway that stretched right across the window, long undusted and tending to buckle. There were seven or eight posts, with six wires on each side of the post. Though I could not think why Constantin wanted them, and though in the event he did not get them, the appearance of them, and of the rusty track beneath them, is all that remains clear in my memory of that window.

'I doubt whether they're for sale,' said my father. 'Look again. There's a good boy. No hurry.'

'They're all I want,' said Constantin, and turned his back on the uninspiring display.

'Well, we'll see,' said my father. 'I'll make a special point of it with the man. . . .' He turned to me. 'And what about you? Very few dolls, I'm afraid.'

'I don't like dolls any more.' As a matter of fact, I had never owned a proper one, although I suffered from this fact when competing with other girls, which meant very seldom, for our friends were few and occasional. The dolls in the window were fly-blown and detestable.

'I think we could find a better shop from which to give Lene a birthday present,' said my mother, in her correct, dignified English.

'We must not be unjust,' said my father, 'when we have not even looked inside.'

The inferiority of the goods implied cheapness, which unfortunately always mattered; although, as it happened, none of the articles seemed actually to be priced.

'I do not like this shop,' said my mother. 'It is a shop that has died.'

Her regal manner when she said such things was, I think, too Germanic for my father's Englishness. That, and the prospect of unexpected economy, perhaps led him to be firm.

'We have Constantin's present to consider as well as Lene's. Let us go in.'

By contrast with the blazing highway, the main impression of the interior was darkness. After a few moments, I also became aware of a smell.

Everything in the shop smelt of that smell, and, one felt, always would do so, the mixed odour of any general store, but at once enhanced and passé. I can smell it now.

'We do not necessarily want to buy anything,' said my father, 'but, if we may, should like to look round?'

Since the days of Mr. Selfridge the proposition is supposed to be taken for granted, but at that time the message had yet to spread. The bazaar keeper seemed hardly to welcome it. He was younger than I had expected (an unusual thing for a child, but I had probably been awaiting a white-bearded gnome); though pale, nearly bald, and perceptibly grimy. He wore an untidy grey suit and bedroom slippers.

'Look about you, children,' said my father. 'Take your time. We can't buy presents every day.'

I noticed that my mother still stood in the doorway.

'I want those wires,' said Constantin.

'Make quite sure by looking at the other things first.'

Constantin turned aside bored, his book held behind his back. He began to scrape his feet. It was up to me to uphold my father's position. Rather timidly, I began to peer about, not going far from him. The bazaar keeper silently watched me with eyes colourless in the twilight.

'Those toy telegraph poles in your window,' said my father after a pause, fraught for me with anxiety and responsibility. 'How much would you take for them?'

'They are not for sale,' said the bazaar keeper, and said no more.

'Then why do you display them in the window?'

'They are a kind of decoration, I suppose.' Did he not know? I wondered.

'Even if they're not normally for sale, perhaps you'll sell them to me,' said my vagabond father, smiling like Rothschild. 'My son, you see, has taken a special fancy to them.'

'Sorry,' said the man in the shop.

'Are you the principal here?'

'I am.'

'Then surely as a reasonable man,' said my father, switching from superiority to ingratiation.

'They are to dress the window,' said the bazaar man. 'They are not for sale.'

This dialogue entered through the back of my head as, diligently and unobtrudingly, I conned the musty stock. At the back of the shop was a window, curtained all over in grey lace: to judge by the weak light it offered, it gave on to the living quarters. Through this much filtered illumination glimmered the façade of an enormous dolls' house. I wanted it at once. Dolls had never been central to my happiness, but this abode of theirs was the most grown-up thing in the shop.

It had battlements, and long straight walls, and a variety of pointed windows. A gothic revival house, no doubt; or even mansion. It was painted the colour of stone; a grey stone darker than the grey light, which flickered round it. There was a two-leaved front door, with a small classical portico. It was impossible to see the whole house at once, as it stood grimed and neglected on the corner of the wide trestle-shelf. Very slowly I walked along two of the sides; the other two being dark against the walls of the shop. From the first-floor window in the side not immediately visible as one approached, leaned a doll, droopy and unkempt. It was unlike any real house I had seen, and, as for dolls' houses, they were always after the style of the villa near Gerrard's Cross belonging to my father's successful brother. My uncle's house itself looked much more like a toy than this austere structure before me.

'Wake up,' said my mother's voice. She was standing just behind me.

'What about some light on the subject?' enquired my father.

A switch clicked.

The house really was magnificent. Obviously, beyond all financial reach.

'Looks like a model for Pentonville Gaol,' observed my father.

'It is beautiful,' I said. 'It's what I want.'

'It's the most depressing-looking plaything I ever saw.'

'I want to pretend I live in it,' I said, 'and give masked balls.' My social history was eager but indiscriminate.

'How much is it?' asked my mother. The bazaar keeper stood resentfully in the background, sliding each hand between the thumb and fingers of the other.

'It's only second-hand,' he said. 'Tenth-hand, more like. A lady brought it in and said she needed to get rid of it. I don't want to sell you something you don't want.'

'But suppose we *do* want it?' said my father truculently. 'Is nothing in this shop for sale?'

'You can take it away for a quid,' said the bazaar keeper. 'And glad to have the space.'

'There's someone looking out,' said Constantin. He seemed to be assessing the house, like a surveyor or valuer.

'It's full of dolls,' said the bazaar keeper. 'They're thrown in. Sure you can transport it?'

'Not at the moment,' said my father, 'but I'll send someone down.' This, I knew, would be Moon the seedman, who owned a large canvas-topped lorry, and with whom my father used to fraternise on the putting green.

'Are you quite sure?' my mother asked me.

'Will it take up too much room?'

My mother shook her head. Indeed, our home, though out of date and out at elbows, was considerably too large for us.

'Then, please.'

Poor Constantin got nothing.

Mercifully, all our rooms had wide doors, so that Moon's driver, assisted by the youth out of the shop, lent specially for the purpose, could ease my birthday present to its new resting place without tilting it or inflicting a wound upon my mother's new and self-applied paint. I noticed that the doll at the first-floor side window had prudently withdrawn.

For my house, my parents had allotted me the principal spare room, because in the centre of it stood a very large dinner table, once to be found in the servants' hall of my father's childhood home in Lincolnshire, but now the sole furniture our principal spare room contained. (The two lesser spare rooms were filled with cardboard boxes, which every now and then toppled in heart-arresting avalanches on still summer nights.) On the big table the driver and the shop boy set my house. It reached almost to the sides, so that those passing along the narrow walks would be in peril of tumbling into a gulf; but, the table being much longer than it was wide, the house was provided at front and back with splendid parterres of deal, embrocated with caustic until they glinted like fluorspar.

When I had settled upon the exact site for the house, so that the garden front would receive the sun from the two windows, and a longer parterre stretched at the front than at the back, where the columned entry faced the door of the room, I withdrew to a distant corner while the two males eased the edifice into exact alignment.

'Snug as a bug in a rug,' said Moon's driver when

the perilous walks at the sides of the house had been made straight and equal.

'Snugger,' said Moon's boy.

I waited for their boots, mailed with crescent silvers of steel, to reach the bottom of our creaking, coconut-matted stair, then I tiptoed to the landing, looked, and listened. The sun had gone in just before the lorry arrived, and down the passage the motes had ceased to dance. It was three o'clock, my mother was still at one of her schools, my father was at the rifle range. I heard the men shut the back door. The principal spare room had never before been occupied, so that the key was outside. In a second, I transferred it to the inside, and shut and locked myself in.

As before in the shop, I walked slowly round my house, but this time round all four sides of it. Then, with the knuckles of my thin white forefinger, I tapped gently at the front door. It seemed not to have been secured, because it opened, both leaves of it, as I touched it. I pried in, first with one eye, then with the other. The lights from various of the pointed windows blotched the walls and floor of the miniature Entrance Hall. None of the dolls was visible.

It was not one of those dolls' houses of commerce from which sides can be lifted in their entirety. To learn about my house, it would be necessary, albeit impolite, to stare through the windows, one at a time. I decided first to take the ground floor. I started in a clockwise direction from the front portico. The front door was still open, but I could not see how to shut it from the outside.

There was a room to the right of the Hall, leading into two other rooms along the right side of the house, of which, again, one led into the other. All the rooms were decorated and furnished in a Mrs. Fitzherbert-ish style; with handsomely striped wallpapers, botanical carpets, and chairs with legs like sticks of brittle golden sweetmeat. There were a number of pictures. I knew just what they were: family portraits. I named the room next the Hall, the Occasional Room, and the room beyond it, the Morning Room. The third room was very small: striking out confidently, I named it the Canton Cabinet, although it contained neither porcelain nor fans. I knew what the rooms in a great house should be called, because my mother used to show me the pictures in large, once-fashionable volumes on the subject which my father had bought for their bulk at junk shops.

Then came the Long Drawing Room, which stretched across the entire garden front of the house, and contained the principal concourse of dolls. It had four pointed French windows, all made to open, though now sealed with dust and rust; above which were bulbous triangles of coloured glass, in tiny snowflake panes. The apartment itself played at being a cloister in a Horace Walpole convent; lierne vaulting ramified across the arched ceiling, and the spidery gothic pilasters were tricked out in mediaeval patchwork, as in a Puseyite church. On the stout golden wallpaper were decent Swiss pastels of indeterminate subjects. There was a grand piano, very black, scrolly, and, no doubt, resounding; four shapely chandeliers; a baronial fireplace with a mythical blazon above the mantel; and eight dolls, all of them female, dotted about on chairs and ottomans with their backs to me. I hardly dared to breathe as I regarded their woolly heads, and noted the colours of their hair: two black, two nondescript, one grey, one a discoloured silver beneath the dust, one blonde, and one a dyed-looking red. They wore woollen Victorian clothes, of a period later, I should say, than that when the house was built, and certainly too warm for the present season; in varied colours, all of them dull. Happy people, I felt even then, would not wear these variants of rust, indigo, and greenwood.

I crept onwards; to the Dining Room. It occupied half its side of the house, and was dark and oppressive. Perhaps it might look more inviting when the chandelier blazed, and the table candles, each with a tiny purple shade, were lighted. There was no cloth on the table, and no food or drink. Over the fireplace was a big portrait of a furious old man: his white hair was a spiky aureole round his distorted face, beetroot-red with rage; the mouth was open, and even the heavy lips were drawn back to show the savage, strong teeth; he was brandishing a very thick walking stick, which seemed to leap from the picture and stun the beholder. He was dressed neutrally, and the painter had not provided him with a background: there was only the aggressive figure menacing the room. I was frightened.

Two rooms on the ground floor remained before I once more reached the front door. In the first of them a lady was writing with her back to the light and therefore to me. She frightened me also; because her grey hair was disordered and of uneven length, and descended in matted plaits, like snakes escaping from a basket, to the shoulders of her coarse grey dress. Of course, being a doll, she did not move, but the back of her head looked mad. Her presence prevented me from regarding at all closely the furnishings of the Writing Room.

Back at the north front, as I resolved to call it, perhaps superseding the compass rather than leading it, there was a cold-looking room, with a carpetless stone floor and white walls, upon which were the mounted heads and horns of many animals. They were all the room contained, but they covered the walls from floor to ceiling. I felt sure that the ferocious old man in the Dining Room had killed all these creatures, and I hated him for it. But I knew what the room would be called: it would be the Trophy Room.

Then I realised that there was no kitchen. It could hardly be upstairs. I had never heard of such a thing. But I looked.

It wasn't there. All the rooms on the first floor were bedrooms. There were six of them, and they so resembled one another, all with dark ochreous wallpaper and narrow brass bedsteads corroded with neglect, that I found it impracticable to distinguish them other than by numbers, at least for the present. Ultimately I might know the house better. Bedrooms 2, 3 and 6 contained two beds each. I recalled that at least nine people lived in the house. In one room the dark walls, the dark floor, the bed linen, and even the glass in the window were splashed, smeared, and further darkened with ink: it seemed apparent who slept there.

I sat on an orange box and looked. My house needed painting and dusting and scrubbing and polishing and renewing; but on the whole I was relieved that things were not worse. I had felt that the house had stood in the dark corner of the shop for no one knew how long, but this, I now saw, could hardly have been true. I wondered about the lady who had needed to get rid of it. Despite that need, she must have kept things up pretty thoroughly. How did she do it? How did she get in? I resolved to ask my mother's advice. I determined to be a good landlord, although, like most who so resolve, my resources were nil. We simply lacked the money to regild my Long Drawing Room in proper gold leaf. But I would bring life to the nine dolls now drooping with boredom and neglect . . .

Then I recalled something. What had become of the doll who had been sagging from the window? I thought she must have been jolted out, and felt myself a murderess. But none of the windows was open. The sash might easily have descended with the shaking; but more probably the poor doll lay inside on the floor of her room. I again went round from room to room, this time on tiptoe, but it was impossible to see the areas of floor just below the dark windows. . . . It was not merely sunless outside, but heavily overcast. I unlocked the door of our principal spare room and descended pensively to await my mother's return and tea.

Wormwood Grange, my father called my house, with penological associations still on his mind. (After he was run over, I realised for the first time that there might be a reason for this, and for his inability to find work worthy of him.) My mother had made the most careful inspection on my behalf, but had been unable to suggest any way of making an entry, or at least of passing beyond the Hall, to which the front doors still lay open. There seemed no question of whole walls lifting off, of the roof being removable, or even of a window being opened, including, mysteriously, on the first floor.

'I don't think it's meant for children, Liebchen,' said my Mother, smiling her lovely smile. 'We shall have to consult the Victoria and Albert Museum.'

'Of course it's not meant for children,' I replied. 'That's why I wanted it. I'm going to receive, like La Belle Otero.'

Next morning, after my mother had gone to work, my father came up, and wrenched and prodded with his unskilful hands.

'I'll get a chisel,' he said. 'We'll prise it open at each corner, and when we've got the fronts off, I'll go over to Woolworths and buy some hinges and screws. I expect they'll have some.'

At that I struck my father in the chest with my fist. He seized my wrists, and I screamed that he was not to lay a finger on my beautiful house, that he would be sure to spoil it, that force never got anyone anywhere. I knew my father: when he took an idea for using tools into his head, the only hope for one's property lay in a scene, and in the implication of tears without end in the future, if the idea were not dropped.

While I was screaming and raving, Constantin appeared from the room below, where he worked at his books.

'Give us a chance, Sis,' he said. 'How can I keep it all in my head about the Thirty Years War when you haven't learned to control your tantrums?'

Although two years younger than I, Constantin should have known that I was past the age for screaming except of set purpose.

'You wait until he tries to rebind all your books, you silly sneak,' I yelled at him.

My father released my wrists.

'Wormwood Grange can keep,' he said. 'I'll think of something else to go over to Woolworths for.' He sauntered off.

Constantin nodded gravely. 'I understand,' he said. 'I understand what you mean. I'll go back to my work. Here, try this.' He gave me a small, chipped nail file.

I spent most of the morning fiddling very cautiously with the imperfect jemmy, and trying to make up my mind about the doll at the window.

I failed to get into my house, and I refused to let my parents give me any effective aid. Perhaps by now I did not really want to get in, although the dirt and disrepair, and the apathy of the dolls, who so badly needed plumping up and dispersing, continued to cause me distress. Certainly I spent as long trying to shut the front door as trying to open a window or find a concealed spring (that idea was Constantin's). In the end I wedged the two halves of the front door with two halves of match; but I felt that the arrangement was makeshift and undignified. I refused everyone access to the principal spare room until something more appropriate could be evolved. My plans for routs and orgies had to be deferred: one could hardly riot among dust and cobwebs.

Then I began to have dreams about my house, and about its occupants.

One of the oddest dreams was the first. It was three or four days after I entered into possession. During that time it had remained cloudy and oppressive, so that my father took to leaving off his knitted waistcoat; then suddenly it thundered. It was a long, slow, distant, intermittent thunder; and it continued all the evening, until, when it was quite dark, my bedtime and Constantin's could no longer be deferred.

'Your ears will get accustomed to the noise,' said my father. 'Just try to take no notice of it.'

Constantin looked dubious; but I was tired of the slow, rumbling hours, and ready for the different dimension of dreams.

I slept almost immediately, although the thunder was rolling round my big, rather empty bedroom, round the four walls, across the floor, and under the ceiling, weighting the black air as with a smoky vapour. Occasionally, the lightning glinted, pink and green. It was still the long-drawn-out preliminary to a storm; the tedious, imperfect dispersal of the accumulated energy of the summer. The rollings and rumblings entered my dreams, which flickered, changed, were gone as soon as come, failed, like the lightning, to concentrate or strike home, were as difficult to profit by as the events of an average day.

After exhausting hours of phantasmagoria, anticipating so many later nights in my life, I found myself in a black wood, with huge, dense trees. I was following a path, but reeled from tree to tree, bruising and cutting myself on their hardness and roughness. There seemed no end to the wood or to the night; but suddenly, in the thick of both, I came upon my house. It stood solid, immense, hemmed in, with a single light, little more, it seemed, than a night-light, burning in every upstairs window (as often in dreams, I could see all four sides of the house at once), and illuminating two wooden wedges, jagged and swollen, which held tight the front doors. The vast trees dipped and swayed their elephantine boughs over the roof; the wind peeked and creaked through the black battlements. Then there was a blaze of whitest lightning, proclaiming the storm itself. In the second it endured, I saw my two wedges fly through the air and the double front door burst open.

For the hundredth time, the scene changed, and now I was back in my room, though still asleep or half-asleep, still dragged from vision to vision. Now the thunder was coming in immense, calculated bombardments; the lightning ceaseless and searing the face of the earth. From being a weariness the storm had become an ecstasy. It seemed as if the whole world would be in dissolution before the thunder had spent its impersonal, unregarding strength. But, as I say, I must still have been at least half-asleep, because between the fortissimi and the lustre I still from time to time saw scenes, meaningless or nightmarish, which could not be found in the wakeful world; still, between and through the volleys, heard impossible sounds.

I do not know whether I was asleep or awake when the storm rippled into tranquillity. I certainly did not feel that the air had been cleared; but this may have been because, surprisingly, I heard a quick soft step passing along the passage outside my room, a passage uncarpeted through our poverty. I well knew all the footsteps in the house, and this was none of them.

Always one to meet trouble half-way, I dashed in my nightgown to open the door. I looked out. The dawn was seeping, without effort or momentum, through every cranny, and showed shadowy the back of a retreating figure, the size of my mother but with woolly red hair and long rust-coloured dress. The padding feet seemed actually to start soft echoes amid all that naked woodwork. I had no need to consider who she was or whither she was bound. I burst into the purposeless tears I so despised.

In the morning, and before deciding upon what to impart, I took Constantin with me to look at the house. I more than half-expected big changes; but none was to be seen. The sections of match-stick were still in position, and the dolls as inactive and diminutive as ever, sitting with their backs to me on chairs and sofas in the Long Drawing Room; their hair dusty, possibly even mothy. Constantin looked at me curiously, but I imparted nothing.

Other dreams followed; though at considerable intervals. Many children have recurring nightmares of oppressive realism and terrifying content;

and I realised from past experience that I must outgrow the habit or lose my house – my house at least. It is true that my house now frightened me, but I felt that I must not be foolish and should strive to take a grown-up view of painted woodwork and nine understuffed dolls. Still it was bad when I began to hear them in the darkness; some tapping, some stumping, some creeping, and therefore not one, but many, or all; and worse when I began not to sleep for fear of the mad doll (as I was sure she was) doing something mad, although I refused to think what. I never dared again to look; but when something happened, which, as I say, was only at intervals (and to me, being young, they seemed long intervals), I lay taut and straining among the forgotten sheets. Moreover, the steps themselves were never quite constant, certainly too inconstant to report to others; and I am not sure that I should have heard anything significant if I had not once seen. But now I locked the door of our principal spare room on the outside, and altogether ceased to visit my beautiful, impregnable mansion.

I noticed that my mother made no comment. But one day my father complained of my ingratitude in never playing with my handsome birthday present. I said I was occupied with my holiday task: *Moby Dick*. This was an approved answer, and even, as far as it went, a true one, though I found the book pointless in the extreme, and horribly cruel.

'I told you the Grange was the wrong thing to buy,' said my father. 'Morbid sort of object for a toy.'

'None of us can learn except by experience,' said my mother.

My father said, 'Not at all,' and bristled.

All this, naturally, was in the holidays. I was going at the time to one of my mother's schools, where I should stay until I could begin to train as a dancer, upon which I was conventionally but entirely resolved. Constantin went to another, a highly cerebral co-educational place, where he would remain until, inevitably, he won a scholarship to a University, perhaps a foreign one. Despite our years, we went our different ways dangerously on small dingy bicycles. We reached home at assorted hours, mine being the longer journey.

One day I returned to find our dining-room table littered with peculiarly uninteresting printed drawings. I could make nothing of them whatever (they did not seem even to belong to the kind of geometry I was – regretfully – used to); and they curled up on themselves when one tried to examine them, and bit one's finger. My father had a week or two before taking one of his infrequent jobs; night work of some kind a long way off, to which he had now departed in our car. Obviously the drawings were connected with Constantin, but he was not there.

I went upstairs, and saw that the principal spare room door was open. Constantin was inside. There had, of course, been no question of the key to the room being removed. It was only necessary to turn it.

'Hallo, Lene,' Constantin said in his matter-of-fact way. 'We've been doing axonometric projection, and I'm projecting your house.' He was making one of the drawings; on a sheet of thick white paper.

'It's for home-work. It'll knock out all the others. They've got to do their real houses.'

It must not be supposed that I did not like Constantin, although often he annoyed me with his placidity and precision. It was weeks since I had seen my house, and it looked unexpectedly interesting. A curious thing happened: nor was it the last time in my life that I experienced it. Temporarily I became a different person; confident, practical, simple. The clear evening sun of autumn may have contributed.

'I'll help,' I said. 'Tell me what to do.'

'It's a bore I can't get in to take measurements. Although we haven't *got* to. In fact, the Clot told us not. Just a general impression, he said. It's to give us the *concept* of axonometry. But, golly, it would be simpler with feet and inches.'

To judge by the amount of white paper he had covered in what could only have been a short time, Constantin seemed to me to be doing very well, but he was one never to be content with less than perfection.

'Tell me', I said, 'what to do, and I'll do it.'

'Thanks,' he replied, sharpening his pencil with a special instrument. 'But it's a one-man job this. In the nature of the case. Later I'll show you how to do it, and you can do some other building if you like.'

I remained, looking at my house and fingering it, until Constantin made it clearer that I was a distraction. I went away, changed my shoes, and put on the kettle against my mother's arrival, and our High Tea.

When Constantin came down (my mother had called for him three times, but that was not unusual), he said, 'I say, Sis, here's a rum thing.'

My mother said, 'Don't use slang, and don't call your sister Sis.'

He said, as he always did when reproved by her, 'I'm sorry, Mother.' Then he thrust the drawing paper at me. 'Look, there's a bit missing. See what I mean?' He was showing me with his stub of emerald pencil, pocked with toothmarks.

Of course, I didn't see. I didn't understand a thing about it.

'After Tea,' said my mother. She gave to such familiar words not a maternal but an imperial decisiveness.

'But Mum–' pleaded Constantin.

'Mother,' said my mother.

Constantin started dipping for sauerkraut.

Silently we ate ourselves into tranquillity; or, for me, into the appearance of it. My alternative personality, though it had survived Constantin's refusal of my assistant, was now beginning to ebb.

'What is all this that you are doing?' enquired my mother in the end. 'It resembles the Stone of Rosetta.'

'I'm taking an axonometric cast of Lene's birthday house.'

'And so?'

But Constantin was not now going to expound immediately. He put in his mouth a finger of rye bread smeared with homemade cheese. Then he said quietly, 'I got down a rough idea of the house, but the rooms don't fit. At least, they don't on the bottom floor. It's all right, I think, on the top floor. In

fact that's the rummest thing of all. Sorry, Mother.'
He had been speaking with his mouth full, and now
filled it fuller.

'What nonsense is this?' To me it seemed that
my mother was glaring at him in a way most unlike
her.

'It's not nonsense, Mother. Of course, I haven't
measured the place, because you can't. But I haven't
done axonometry for nothing. There's a part of the bottom floor I can't get at. A secret room or something.'

'Show me.'

'Very well, Mother.' Constantin put down his
remnant of bread and cheese. He rose, looking a
little pale. He took the drawing round the table to
my mother.

'Not that thing. I can't understand it, and I don't
believe you can understand it either.' Only sometimes to my father did my mother speak like that.
'Show me in the house.'

I rose too.

'You stay here, Lene. Put some more water in the
kettle and boil it.'

'But it's my house. I have a right to know.'

My mother's expression changed to one more familiar. 'Yes, Lene,' she said, 'you have a right. But please not now. I ask you.'

I smiled at her and picked up the kettle.

'Come, Constantin.'

I lingered by the kettle in the kitchen, not wishing to give an impression of eavesdropping or even undue eagerness, which I knew would distress my mother. I never wished to learn things that my mother wished to keep from me, and I never questioned her implication of 'All in good time'.

But they were not gone long, for well before the kettle had begun even to grunt, my mother's beautiful voice was summoning me back.

'Constantin is quite right,' she said, when I had presented myself at the dining room table, 'and it was wrong of me to doubt it. The house is built in a funny sort of way. But what does it matter?'

Constantin was not eating.

39

'I am glad that you are studying well, and learning such useful things,' said my mother.

She wished the subject to be dropped, and we dropped it.

Indeed, it was difficult to think what more could be said. But I waited for a moment in which I was alone with Constantin. My father's unhabitual absence made this difficult, and it was completely dark before the moment came.

And when, as was only to be expected, Constantin had nothing to add, I felt, most unreasonably, that he was joined with my mother in keeping something from me.

'But what *happened*?' I pressed him. 'What happened when you were in the room with her?'

'What do you think happened?' replied Constantin, wishing, I thought, that my mother would re-enter. 'Mother realised that I was right. Nothing more. What does it matter anyway?'

That final query confirmed my doubts.

'Constantin,' I said. 'Is there anything I ought to do?'

'Better hack the place open,' he answered, almost irritably.

But a most unexpected thing happened, that, had I even considered adopting Constantin's idea, would have saved me the trouble. When next day I returned from school, my house was gone.

Constantin was sitting in his usual corner, this time absorbing Greek paradigms. Without speaking to him (nothing unusual in that when he was working), I went straight to the principal spare room. The vast deal table, less scrubbed than once, was bare. The place where my house had stood was very visible, as if indeed a palace had been swept off by a djinn. But I could see no other sign of its passing: no scratched woodwork, or marks of boots, or disjoined fragments.

Constantin seemed genuinely astonished at the news. But I doubted him.

'You knew,' I said.

'Of course I didn't know.'

Still, he understood what I was thinking.

He said again, 'I didn't know.'

Unlike me on occasion, he always spoke the truth.

I gathered myself together and blurted out, 'Have they done it themselves?' Inevitably I was frightened, but in a way I was also relieved.

'Who do you mean?'

'They.'

I was inviting ridicule, but Constantin was kind.

He said, 'I know who I think has done it, but you mustn't let on. I think Mother's done it.'

I did not again enquire uselessly into how much more he knew than I. I said, 'But *how*?'

Constantin shrugged. It was a habit he had assimilated with so much else.

'Mother left the house with us this morning and she isn't back yet.'

'She must have put Father up to it.'

'But there are no marks.'

'Father might have got help.' There was a pause. Then Constantin said, 'Are you sorry?'

'In a way,' I replied. Constantin with precocious wisdom left it at that.

When my mother returned, she simply said that my father had already lost his new job, so that we had had to sell things.

'I hope you will forgive your father and me,' she said. 'We've had to sell one of my watches also. Father will soon be back to Tea.'

She too was one I had never known to lie; but now I began to perceive how relative and instrumental truth could be.

I need not say: not in those terms. Such clear concepts, with all they offer of gain and loss, come later, if they come at all. In fact, I need not say that the whole of what goes before is so heavily filtered through later experience as to be of little evidential value. But I am scarcely putting forward evidence. There is so little. All I can do is to tell something of what happened, as it now seems to me to have been.

I remember sulking at my mother's news, and her explaining to me that really I no longer liked the house and that something better would be bought for me in replacement when our funds permitted.

I did ask my father when he returned to our evening meal, whistling and falsely jaunty about the lost job, how much he had been paid for my house.

'A trifle more than I gave for it. That's only business.'

'Where is it now?'

'Never you mind.'

'Tell her,' said Constantin. 'She wants to know.'

'Eat your herring,' said my father very sharply. 'And mind your own business.'

And, thus, before long my house was forgotten, my occasional nightmares returned to earlier themes.

It was, as I say, for two or three months in 1921 that I owned the house and from time to time dreamed that creatures I supposed to be its occupants had somehow invaded my home. The next thirty years, more or less, can be disposed of quickly: It was the period when I tried conclusions with the outer world.

I really became a dancer; and, although the upper reaches alike of the art and of the profession notably eluded me, yet I managed to maintain myself for several years, no small achievement. I retired, as they say, upon marriage. My husband aroused physical passion in me for the first time, but diminished and deadened much else. He was reported missing in the late misguided war. Certainly he did not return to me. I at least still miss him, though often I despise myself for doing so.

My father died in a street accident when I was fifteen: It happened on the day I received a special commendation from the sallow Frenchwoman who taught me to dance. After his death my beloved mother always wanted to return to Germany. Before long I was spiritually self-sufficient enough, or said I was, to make that possible. Unfailingly, she wrote to me twice a week, although to find words in which to reply was often difficult for me. Sometimes I visited her, while the conditions in her country became more and more uncongenial to me. She had a fair position teaching English Language and Literature at a small university; and she seemed increasingly to be infected by the new notions and emotions raging around her. I must acknowledge that sometimes their tumult and intoxication unsteadied my own mental gait, although I was a foreigner and by no means of sanguine temperament. It is a mistake to think that all professional dancers are gay.

Despite what appeared to be increasing sympathies with the new regime, my mother disappeared. She was the first of the two people who mattered to me in such very different ways, and who so unreasonably vanished. For a time I was ill, and of course I love her still more than anybody. If she had remained with me, I am sure I should never have married. Without involving myself in psychology, which I detest, I shall simply say that the thought and recollection of my mother lay, I believe, behind the self-absorption my husband complained of so bitterly and so justly. It was not really myself in which I was absorbed but the memory of perfection. It is the plain truth that such beauty, and goodness, and depth, and capacity for love were my mother's alone.

Constantin abandoned all his versatile reading and became a priest, in fact a member of the Society of Jesus. He seems exalted (possibly too much so for his colleagues and superiors), but I can no longer speak to him or bear his presence. He frightens me. Poor Constantin!

On the other hand, I, always dubious, have become a complete unbeliever. I cannot see that Constantin is doing anything but listening to his own inner voice (which has changed its tone since we were children); and mine speaks a different language. In the long run, I doubt whether there is much to be desired but death; or whether there is endurance in anything but suffering. I no longer see myself feasting crowned heads on quails.

So much for biographical intermission. I proceed to the circumstances of my second and recent experience of landlordism.

In the first place, I did something thoroughly stupid. Instead of following the road marked on the map, I took a short cut. It is true that the short cut was shown on the map also, but the region was much too unfrequented for a wandering footpath to be in any way dependable, especially in this generation which has ceased to walk beyond the garage or the bus stop. It was one of the least populated districts in the whole country, and, moreover, the slow autumn dusk was already perceptible when I pushed at the first, dilapidated gate.

To begin with, the path trickled and flickered across a sequence of small damp meadows, bearing neither cattle nor crop. When it came to the third or fourth of these meadows, the way had all but vanished in the increasing sogginess, and could be continued only by looking for the stile or gate in the unkempt hedge ahead. This was not especially difficult as long as the fields remained small; but after a time I reached a depressing expanse which could hardly be termed a field at all, but was rather a large marsh. It was at this point that I should have returned and set about tramping the winding road.

But a path of some kind again continued before me, and I perceived that the escapade had already consumed twenty minutes. So I risked it, although soon I was striding laboriously from tussock to brown tussock in order not to sink above my shoes into the surrounding quagmire. It is quite extraordinary how far one can stray from a straight or determined course when thus preoccupied with elementary comfort. The hedge on the far side of the marsh was still a long way ahead, and the tussocks themselves were becoming both less frequent and less dense, so that too often I was sinking through them into the mire. I realised that the marsh sloped slightly downwards in the direction I was following, so that before I reached the hedge, I might have to cross a river. In the event, it was not so much a river as an indeterminately bounded augmentation of the softness, and moistness, and ooziness: I struggled across, jerking from false foothold to palpable pit-fall, and before long despairing even of the attempt to step securely. Both my feet were now soaked to well above the ankles, and the visibility had become less than was entirely convenient.

When I reached what I had taken for a hedge, it proved to be the boundary of an extensive thicket.

Autumn had infected much of the greenery with blotched and dropping senility; so that bare brown briars arched and tousled, and purple thorns tilted at all possible angles for blood. To go further would demand an axe. Either I must retraverse the dreary bog in the perceptibly waning light, or I must skirt the edge and seek an opening in the thicket. Undecided, I looked back. I realised that I had lost the gate through which I had entered upon the marsh on the other side. There was nothing to do but creep as best I could upon the still treacherous ground along the barrier of dead dog-roses, mildewed blackberries, and rampant nettles.

But it was not long before I reached a considerable gap, from which through the tangled vegetation seemed to lead a substantial track, although by no means a straight one. The track wound on unimpeded for a considerable distance, even becoming firmer underfoot; until I realised that the thicket had become an entirely indisputable wood. The brambles clutching maliciously from the sides had become watching branches above my head. I could not recall that the map had showed a wood. If, indeed, it had done so, I should not have entered upon the footpath, because the only previous occasion in my life when I had been truly lost, in the sense of being unable to find the way back as well as being unable to go on, had been when my father had once so effectively lost us in a wood that I have never again felt the same about woods. The fear I had felt for perhaps an hour and a half on that occasion, though told to no one, and swiftly evaporating from consciousness upon our emergence, had been the veritable fear of death. Now I drew the map from where it lay against my thigh in the big pocket of my dress. It was not until I tried to read it that I realised how near I was to night. Until it came to print, the problems of the route had given me cat's eyes.

I peered, and there was no wood, no green patch on the map, but only the wavering line of dots advancing across contoured whiteness to the neck of yellow road where the short cut ended. But I did not reach any foolish conclusion. I simply guessed that

I had strayed very badly; the map was spattered with green marks in places where I had no wish to be; and the only question was in which of those many thickets I now was. I could think of no way to find out. I was nearly lost, and this time I could not blame my father.

The track I had been following still stretched ahead, as yet not too indistinct; and I continued to follow it. As the trees around me became yet bigger and thicker, fear came upon me, though not the death fear of that previous occasion, I felt, now that I knew what was going to happen next; or, rather, I felt I knew one thing that was going to happen next, a thing which was but a small and far from central part of an obscure, inapprehensible totality. As one does on such occasions, I felt more than half outside my body. If I continued much further, I might change into somebody else.

But what happened was not what I expected. Suddenly I saw a flicker of light. It seemed to emerge from the left, to weave momentarily among the trees, and to disappear to the right. It was not what I expected, but it was scarcely reassuring. I wondered if it could be a will-o'-the-wisp, a thing I had never seen, but which I understood to be connected with marshes. Next a still more prosaic possibility occurred to me, one positively hopeful: the headlights of a motor car turning a corner. It seemed the likely answer, but my uneasiness did not perceptibly diminish.

I struggled on, and the light came again: a little stronger, and twisting through the trees around me. Of course another car at the same corner of the road was not an impossibility, even though it was an un-peopled area. Then, after a period of soft but not comforting dusk, it came a third time; and, soon, a fourth. There was no sound of an engine: and it seemed to me that the transit of the light was too swift and fleeting for any car.

And then what I had been awaiting happened. I came suddenly upon a huge square house. I had known it was coming, but still it struck at my heart.

It is not every day that one finds a dream come true; and, scared though I was, I noticed details: for example, that there did not seem to be those single lights burning in every upstairs window. Doubtless dreams, like poems, demand a certain licence; and, for the matter of that, I could not see all four sides of the house at once, as I had dreamed I had. But that perhaps was the worst of it: I was plainly not dreaming now.

A sudden greeny-pink radiance illuminated around me a morass of weed and neglect; and then seemed to hide itself among the trees on my right. The explanation of the darting lights was that a storm approached. But it was unlike other lightning I had encountered: being slower, more silent, more regular.

There seemed nothing to do but run away, though even then it seemed sensible not to run back into the wood. In the last memories of daylight, I began to wade through the dead knee-high grass of the lost lawn. It was still possible to see that the wood continued, opaque as ever, in a long line to my left; I felt my way along it, in order to keep as far as possible from the the house. I noticed, as I passed, the great portico, facing the direction from which I had emerged. Then, keeping my distance, I crept along the grey east front with its two tiers of pointed windows, all shut and one or two broken; and reached the southern parterre, visibly vaster, even in the storm-charged gloom, than the northern, but no less ravaged. Ahead, and at the side of the parterre far off to my right, ranged the encircling woodland. If no path manifested, my state would be hazardous indeed; and there seemed little reason for a path, as the approach to the house was provided by that along which I had come from the marsh.

As I struggled onwards, the whole scene was transformed: in a moment the sky became charged with roaring thunder, the earth with tumultuous rain. I tried to shelter in the adjacent wood, but instantly found myself enmeshed in bines and suckers, lacerated by invisible spears. In a minute I should be drenched. I plunged through the wet weeds towards the spreading portico.

Before the big doors I waited for several minutes, watching the lightning, and listening. The rain leapt up where it fell, as if the earth hurt it.

A rising chill made the old grass shiver. It seemed unlikely that anyone could live in a house so dark; but suddenly I heard one of the doors behind me scrape open. I turned. A dark head protruded between the portals, like Punch from the side of his booth.

'Oh.' The shrill voice was of course surprised to see me.

I turned. 'May I please wait until the rain stops?'

'You can't come inside.'

I drew back; so far back that a heavy drip fell on the back of my neck from the edge of the portico. With absurd melodrama, there was a loud roll of thunder.

'I shouldn't think of it,' I said. 'I must be on my way the moment the rain lets me.' I could still see only the round head sticking out between the leaves of the door.

'In the old days we often had visitors.' This statement was made in the tone of a Cheltenham lady remarking that when a child she often spoke to gypsies. 'I only peeped out to see the thunder.'

Now, within the house, I heard another, lower voice, although I could not hear what it said. Through the long crack between the doors, a light slid out across the flagstones of the porch and down the darkening steps.

'She's waiting for the rain to stop,' said the shrill voice.

'Tell her to come in,' said the deep voice. 'Really, Emerald, you forget your manners after all this time.'

'I *have* told her,' said Emerald very petulantly, and withdrawing her head. 'She won't do it.'

'Nonsense,' said the other. 'You're just telling lies.' I got the idea that thus she always spoke to Emerald.

Then the doors opened, and I could see the two of them silhouetted in the light of a lamp which stood on a table behind them; one much the taller, but both with round heads, and both wearing long, unshapely garments. I wanted very much to escape, and failed to do so only because there seemed nowhere to go.

'Please come in at once,' said the taller figure, 'and let us take off your wet clothes.'

'Yes, yes,' squeaked Emerald, unreasonably jubilant.

'Thank you. But my clothes are not at all wet.'

'None the less, please come in. We shall take it as a discourtesy if you refuse.'

Another roar of thunder emphasised the impracticability of continuing to refuse much longer. If this was a dream, doubtless, and to judge by experience, I should awake.

And a dream it must be, because there at the front door were two big wooden wedges; and there to the right of the Hall, shadowed in the lamplight, was the Trophy Room; although now the animal heads on the walls were shoddy, fungoid ruins, their sawdust spilled and clotted on the cracked and uneven flagstones of the floor.

'You must forgive us,' said my tall hostess. 'Our landlord neglects us sadly, and we are far gone in wrack and ruin. In fact, I do not know what we should do were it not for our own resources.' At this

Emerald cackled. Then she came up to me, and began fingering my clothes.

The tall one shut the door.

'Don't touch,' she shouted at Emerald, in her deep, rather grinding voice. 'Keep your fingers off.'

She picked up the large oil lamp. Her hair was a discoloured white in its beams.

'I apologise for my sister,' she said. 'We have all been so neglected that some of us have quite forgotten how to behave. Come, Emerald.'

Pushing Emerald before her, she led the way.

In the Occasional Room and the Morning Room, the gilt had flaked from the gingerbread furniture, the family portraits stared from their heavy frames, and the striped wallpaper drooped in the lamplight like an assembly of sodden, half-inflated balloons.

At the door of the Canton Cabinet, my hostess turned. 'I am taking you to meet my sisters,' she said.

'I look forward to doing so,' I replied, regardless of truth, as in childhood.

She nodded slightly, and proceeded. 'Take care,' she said. 'The floor has weak places.'

In the little Canton Cabinet, the floor had, in fact, largely given way, and been plainly converted into a hospice for rats.

And then, there they all were, the remaining six of them thinly illumined by what must surely be rushlights in the four shapely chandeliers. But now, of course, I could see their faces.

'We are all named after our birthstones,' said my hostess. 'Emerald you know. I am Opal. Here are Diamond and Garnet, Cornelian and Chrysolite. The one with the grey hair is Sardonyx, and the beautiful one is Turquoise.'

They all stood up. During the ceremony of introduction, they made odd little noises.

'Emerald and I are the eldest, and Turquoise of course is the youngest.'

Emerald stood in the corner before me, rolling her dyed-red head. The Long Drawing Room was raddled with decay. The cobwebs gleamed like steel filigree in the beam of the lamp, and the sisters seemed to have been seated in cocoons of them, like cushions of gossamer.

'There is one other sister, Topaz. But she is busy writing.'

'Writing all our diaries,' said Emerald.

'Keeping the record,' said my hostess.

A silence followed.

'Let us sit down,' said my hostess. 'Let us make our visitor welcome.'

The six of them gently creaked and subsided into their former places. Emerald and my hostess remained standing.

'Sit down, Emerald. Our visitor shall have *my* chair as it is the best.' I realised that inevitably there was no extra seat.

'Of course not,' I said. 'I can only stay for a minute. I am waiting for the rain to stop,' I explained feebly to the rest of them.

'I insist,' said my hostess.

I looked at the chair to which she was pointing. The padding was burst and rotten, the woodwork bleached and crumbling to collapse. All of them were watching me with round, vague eyes in their flat faces.

'Really,' I said, 'no, thank you, It's kind of you,

but I must go.' All the same, the surrounding wood and the dark marsh beyond it loomed scarcely less appalling than the house itself and its inmates.

'We should have more to offer, more and better in every way, were it not for our landlord.' She spoke with bitterness, and it seemed to me that on all the faces the expression changed. Emerald came towards me out of her corner, and again began to finger my clothes. But this time her sister did not correct her, and when I stepped away, she stepped after me and went on as before.

'She has failed in the barest duty of sustentation.'

I could not prevent myself starting at the pronoun. At once, Emerald caught hold of my dress, and held it tightly.

'But there is one place she cannot spoil for us. One place where we can entertain in our own way.'

'Please,' I cried. 'Nothing more. I am going now.'

Emerald's pygmy grip tautened.

'It is the room where we eat.'

All the watching eyes lighted up, and became something they had not been before.

'I may almost say where we feast.'

The six of them began again to rise from their spidery bowers.

'Because *she* cannot go there.'

The sisters clapped their hands, like a rustle of leaves.

'There we can be what we really are.'

The eight of them were now grouped round me. I noticed that the one pointed out as the youngest was passing her dry, pointed tongue over her lower lip.

'Nothing unladylike, of course.'

'Of course not,' I agreed.

'But firm,' broke in Emerald, dragging at my dress as she spoke. 'Father said that must always come first.'

'Our father was a man of measureless wrath against a slight,' said my hostess. 'It is his continuing presence about the house which largely upholds us.'

'Shall I show her?' asked Emerald.

'Since you wish to,' said her sister disdainfully.

From somewhere in her musty garments Emerald

produced a scrap of card, which she held out to me.

'Take it in your hand. I'll allow you to hold it.'

It was a photograph, obscurely damaged.

'Hold up the lamp,' squealed Emerald. With an aloof gesture her sister raised it.

It was a photograph of myself when a child, bobbed and waistless. And through my heart was a tiny brown needle.

'We've all got things like it,' said Emerald jubilantly. 'Wouldn't you think her heart would have rusted away by now?'

'She never had a heart,' said the elder sister scornfully, putting down the light.

'She might not have been able to help what she did,' I cried.

I could hear the sisters catch their fragile breath.

'It's what you do that counts,' said my hostess, regarding the discoloured floor, 'not what you feel about it afterwards. Our father always insisted on that. It's obvious.'

'Give it back to me,' said Emerald, staring into my eyes. For a moment I hesitated.

'Give it back to her,' said my hostess in her contemptuous way. 'It makes no difference now. Everyone but Emerald can see that the work is done.'

I returned the card, and Emerald let go of me as she stuffed it away.

'And now will you join us?' asked my hostess. 'In the inner room?' As far as was possible, her manner was almost casual.

'I am sure the rain has stopped,' I replied. 'I must be on my way.'

'Our father would never have let you go so easily, but I think we have done what we can with you.'

I inclined my head.

'Do not trouble with adieux,' she said. 'My sisters no longer expect them.' She picked up the lamp. 'Follow me. And take care. The floor has weak places.'

'Goodbye,' squealed Emerald.

'Take no notice, unless you wish,' said my hostess.

I followed her through the mouldering rooms and across the rotten floors in silence. She opened both

65

the outer doors and stood waiting for me to pass through. Beyond, the moon was shining, and she stood dark and shapeless in the silver flood.

On the threshold, or somewhere on the far side of it, I spoke.

'I did nothing,' I said. 'Nothing,'

So far from replying, she dissolved into the darkness and silently shut the door.

I took up my painful, lost, and forgotten way through the wood, across the dreary marsh, and back to the little yellow road.